Will   Irma   Taranee   Cornelia   Hay Lin

GRAPHIC NOVEL #2

MERIDIAN MAGIC

W.i.t.c.h. 2

Will Irma Taranee Cornelia Hay Lin

GRAPHIC NOVEL #2

MERIDIAN MAGIC

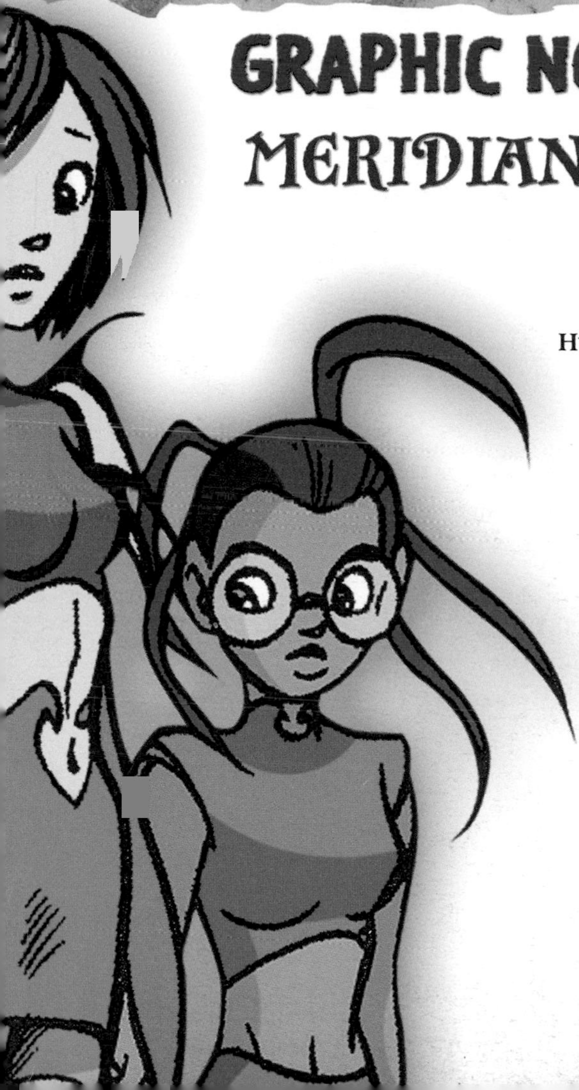

VOLO
an imprint of
HYPERION BOOKS FOR CHILDREN
New York

Printed in the United States of America

First Edition
1 3 5 7 9 10 8 6 4 2

ISBN 0-7868-0974-4

Visit www.clubwitch.com

WHAT WAS THAT SOUND?

IT WAS MY STOMACH, IRMA. I'M STARVING. IT'S LATE. CAN WE PLEASE GO HOME?

FIRST, I WANT TO FIND OUT MRS. RUDOLPH'S SECRETS.

WHAT SECRETS? SHE SPENT THE WHOLE AFTERNOON GRADING OUR MATH TESTS! WHY CAN'T YOU ADMIT YOU WERE WRONG?

MAYBE I WILL, BUT FIRST I WANT TO CHECK, ONE MORE TIME. I JUST GOT AN IDEA! ARE YOU FREE TOMORROW MORNING?

WE ARE SUPPOSED TO BE IN SCHOOL TOMORROW MORNING.

WHATEVER! WE'LL SPEND ALMOST TWENTY YEARS OF OUR LIFE IN SCHOOL! WE CAN TAKE ONE DAY OFF!

YOU ARE GOING TO RUIN ME. WHEN I FLUNK I'LL KNOW WHO I HAVE TO THANK!

BUT WHAT IF THAT WOMAN REALLY IS A MONSTER? DON'T BE SELFISH, HAY LIN! YOU HAVE A CHANCE TO SAVE THE WORLD!

NO! NO! NO! I DON'T WANT TO. . . .

PLEASE CHANGE YOUR MIND.

OH, FOR HEAVEN'S SAKE! YOU KNOW WHAT...

OKAY . . .

. . . NOW WE'RE READY!

47

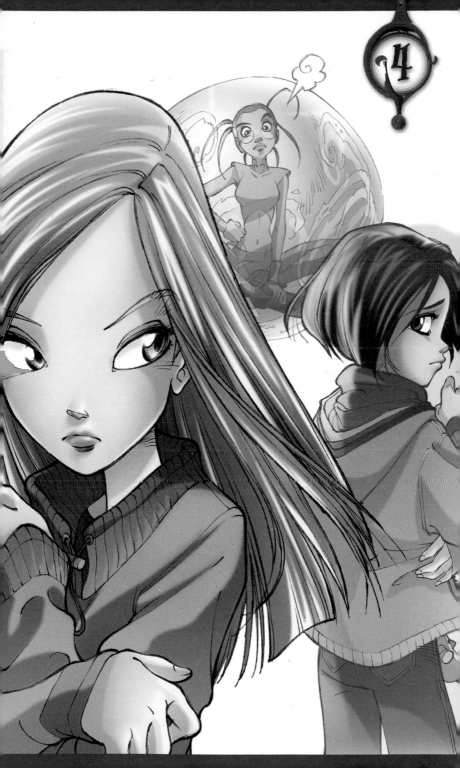

A SMILE

TARANEE SMILES AND HAY LIN CANNOT HELP OBSERVING HER.

BE QUIET, EVERYONE! LET'S CALL THE ROLL!

...RYTHING HAPPENED LIKE ...EAM. THE DISCOVERY OF ... POWERS, THE SADNESS ... GRANDMOTHER'S DEATH, ... TRIP TO METAMOOR. . . .

BENSON!

HERE!

A REALITY THAT LETS US HEAR HER VOICE . . .

...LIN HADN'T SEEN HER FRIEND ...E IN PRISON IN THAT ...IOUS WORLD, SHE WOULD ...AID THAT ...E WAS HERE, ... OF HER.

BUT THE REAL TARANEE HAS BEEN REPLACED BY A PERFECT TWIN. AND THIS IS NOT A DREAM, BUT REALITY.

LIN!

?

63

RUDOLPH'S HOUSE IS NOT FAR AWAY. . . .

SO? WHAT'S HAPPENING?

NOTHING! THE **PORTAL** ISN'T OPENING AGAIN!

AND THE SEAL OF PHOBOS ISN'T DOING ANYTHING, EITHER.

THAT HELPED US GET OUT OF THE METAWORLD, BUT ENTERING IS ANOTHER THING!

WE CAN'T LEAVE TARANEE! WE JUST HAVE TO FIND A PORTAL THAT'S STILL OPEN! RIGHT?

NO NEED TO ASK! HAY LIN, DO YOU HAVE THE **MAP** OF THE PORTALS?

HERE, TAKE IT! BUT I . . . HAVE TO GO!

?!

WHAT'S UP WITH HER?

DON'T KNOW. EVER SINCE WE GOT HERE, SHE'S BEEN A LITTLE ODD!

LOOK! THE HEART OF CANDRACAR . . .

. . . IT'S SHOWING US THE WAY!

69

SINCE YOU'VE JUST MOVED HERE, LET ME INTRODUCE YOU TO THE SHELL CAVE!

WOW! IT'S SO AMAZING!

HAT'S WRONG? VHY ARE YOU SCRATCHING YOURSELF, WILL?

BECAUSE NETTLES HAVE AN ITCHY EFFECT ON ME!

THAT'S NOT AN ANSWER!

ACTUALLY, IT IS AN ANSWER—I'M ALLERGIC TO NETTLES, AND I FELL INTO SOME....

LET'S GET TO WORK, GIRLS!

79

FIRST WE HAVE TO CREATE SOME ASTRAL DROPS THAT WILL TAKE OUR PLACE!

I DON'T KNOW WHEN WE'LL COME BACK! WELL, TO TELL YOU THE TRUTH, I DON'T KNOW IF WE . . .

IS THAT REALLY NECESSARY?

WE WILL COME BACK, CORNELIA! AND WE'LL BRING TARANEE WITH US!

ALL AT HEATHERFIELD'S CLIFF, SHELL CAVE, 8:30 P.M.

YOUR ASTRAL DROP LEFT TOO, HAY LIN?

YES! AND TO BE SAFE, I QUIZZED HER ON ALL MY HABITS.

SHE'LL GO BACK TO MY HOUSE, LIE DOWN IN MY BED, AND PROBABLY EVEN HAVE MY DREAMS!

WHILE WE, ON THE OTHER HAND, ARE ABOUT TO ENTER A WORLD OF NIGHTMARES!

REPEAT THE LIST ONE MORE TIME!

TIME: SEVEN: WAKE UP! TIME: QUARTER PAST SEVEN: SHOWER! TIME: TEN TO EIGHT: KISS MOM, EAT BREAKFAST AND . . .

O.K., O.K.! IF YOU FOLLOW THE INSTRUCTIONS, YOU CAN'T GO WRONG! AND REMEMBER . . .

. . . TO STUDY WHAT I SHOULD DO! I KNOW! YOU WROTE THAT IN BLACK INK!

83

SIGH! I HOPE SHE FINDS HER WAY HOME.

IT'S DO OR DIE, WILL. HURRY UP!

IT'S DARK IN HERE. LUCKILY HAY LIN AND I BROUGHT EQUIPMENT.

I'VE BEEN IN THIS CAVE THOUSANDS OF TIMES, AND I NEVER THOUGHT ABOUT FINDING A PORTAL HERE!

IRMA!

TRUNCK CLUNK

MOTHER! ARE YOU STILL UP?

WHAT ARE YOU DOING HERE? I SAW YOU GO INTO YOUR ROOM BEFORE!

WELL, GOOD NIGHT! I JUST WANTED TO TELL YOU THAT YOU HAVE BEEN VERY KIND!

UM! YOU'RE RIGHT. IN FACT, I'M GOING BACK RIGHT NOW!

WHAT DO YOU MEAN?

YOU WERE VERY KIND TO THAT BOY TODAY, WHEN YOU ACCEPTED HIS DATE. THAT WAS SWEET OF YOU.

FROM WILL'S ROOM, SHE HEARS THE NAME MARTIN!

YES, DORMOUSE! I ALSO HAVE HEARD THAT CRY! IF IT WASN'T SO FAR, I'D SAY THAT IT'S IRMA'S VOICE.

120